I HAVE TO GO!

Story by Robert Munsch

Art by Michael Martchenko

ANNICK PRESS LTD.

Toronto, Canada

Sixth Printing, January 1989

Annick Press gratefully acknowledges
the contributions of The Canada Council
and The Ontario Arts Council

Canadian Cataloguing in Publication Data

Munsch, Robert N., 1945–
  I have to go

(Munsch for kids)
ISBN 0-920303-77-3 (bound) ISBN 0-920303-74-9 (pbk.)

I. Martchenko, Michael. II. Title. III. Series:
Munsch, Robert N., 1945–   . Munsch for kids.

PS8576.U85152 1987   jC813′.54   C86-095072-7
PZ7.M86Ih 1987

Trade distribution in North America by:
Firefly Books Ltd.
250 Sparks Avenue
Willowdale, Ontario
M2H 2S4 Canada

Printed and bound in Canada by D.W. Friesen & Sons, Altona, Manitoba

To Andrew McIsaac of Cookstown, Ontario
and to Andrew Munsch of Guelph, Ontario

One day Andrew's mother and father were taking him to see his grandma and grandpa. Before they put him in the car his mother said, "Andrew, do you have to go pee?"

Andrew said, "No, no, no, no, no."

His father said very slowly and clearly, "Andrew, do you have to go pee?"

"No, no, no, no," said Andrew. "I have decided never to go pee again."

So they put Andrew into the car, fastened his seatbelt and gave him lots of books, and lots of toys, and lots of crayons, and drove off down the road— VAROOMMM. They had been driving for just one minute when Andrew yelled, "I HAVE TO GO PEE!"

"YIKES," said the father.

"OH NO," said the mother.

Then the father said, "Now Andrew wait just 5 minutes. In 5 minutes we will come to a gas station where you can go pee."

Andrew said, "I have to go pee RIGHT NOW!"

So the mother stopped the car—SCREEEEECH. Andrew jumped out of the car and peed behind a bush.

When they got to grandma and grandpa's house Andrew wanted to go out to play. It was snowing and he needed a snowsuit. Before they put on the snowsuit, the mother and the father and the grandma and the grandpa all said, "ANDREW! DO YOU HAVE TO GO PEE?"

Andrew said, "No, no, no, no, no."

So they put on Andrew's snowsuit. It had 5 zippers, 10 buckles and 17 snaps. It took them half an hour to get the snowsuit on.

Andrew walked out into the back yard, threw one snowball and yelled, "I HAVE TO GO PEE."

The father and the mother and the grandma and the grandpa all ran outside, got Andrew out of the snowsuit and carried him to the bathroom.

When Andrew came back down they had a nice long dinner. Then it was time for Andrew to go to bed.

Before they put Andrew into bed, the mother and the father and the grandma and the grandpa all said, "ANDREW! DO YOU HAVE TO GO PEE?"

Andrew said, "No, no, no, no, no."

So his mother gave him a kiss, and his father gave him a kiss, and his grandma gave him a kiss, and his grandpa gave him a kiss.

"Just wait," said the mother, "He's going to yell and say he has to go pee."

"Oh," said the father, "he does it every night. It's driving me crazy."

The grandmother said, "I never had these problems with my children."

They waited 5 minutes, 10 minutes, 15 minutes, 20 minutes.

The father said, "I think he is asleep."

The mother said, "Yes, I think he is asleep."

The grandmother said, "He is definitely asleep and he didn't yell and say he had to go pee."

Then Andrew said, "I wet my bed."

So the mother and the father and the grandma and the grandpa all changed Andrew's bed and Andrew's pajamas. Then the mother gave him a kiss, and the father gave him a kiss, and the grandma gave him a kiss, and the grandpa gave him a kiss, and the grownups all went downstairs.

They waited 5 minutes, 10 minutes, 15 minutes, 20 minutes, and from upstairs Andrew yelled, "GRANDPA, DO YOU HAVE TO GO PEE?"

And grandpa said, "Why yes, I think I do."

Andrew said, "Well, so do I."

So they both went to the bathroom and peed in the toilet, and Andrew did not wet his bed again that night, not even once.

Other books in the Munsch for Kids Series:

The Dark
Mud Puddle
The Paper Bag Princess
The Boy in the Drawer
Jonathan Cleaned Up, then He Heard a Sound
Murmel, Murmel, Murmel
Millicent and the Wind
The Fire Station
Angela's Airplane
David's Father
Mortimer
Thomas' Snowsuit
50 Below Zero
A Promise is A Promise
Moira's Birthday

Three records, ''MUNSCH, Favourite Stories'',
''Murmel, Murmel, MUNSCH'' and ''Love You Forever''
are available from
Kids Records, Toronto, Canada M4M 2E6